D0989548

DATE DUE			

TUSYA AND THE
POT OF GOLD

TUSYA AND THE
POT OF GOLD

From an old Ukrainian Folktale
retold and illustrated by

YAROSLAVA

Atheneum   1973   New York

Copyright © 1971 by Yaroslava Surmach
Library of Congress catalog card number 70-134817
ISBN 0-689-30002-6
Published simultaneously in Canada by
McClelland & Stewart, Ltd.
Printed by Sir Joseph Causton & Sons, Ltd.
London and Eastleigh, England
Bound by H. Wolff, New York
First Printing August 1971
Second Printing April 1973

For my father, Myron Surmach

L ong ago and farther away than can be told, there lived a poor farmer and his wife. Tomas and Tusya they were called. Tomas worked hard for a rich landowner, but he earned very little. Tusya was a good woman, who managed very well on what little they had. But she had one great fault. She was a gossip. Whatever her husband told her was soon known throughout the village. Nothing Tomas could do or say would stop her tattling tongue.

It happened then one morning as Tomas was plowing a field, that he found a great pot of gold. He knew at once if word of his find got to the landowner or to his steward, one of them would claim the money. Yet there seemed no way to keep them from knowing. As soon as Tusya knew, everyone must know. And the gold would be gone.

Tomas was worried. He had to discover some
way to keep Tusya from telling of the gold.
And at last he worked out a plan.

First he hid the gold where no one would
find it. He said nothing of it to anyone, not even
to Tusya. Then early the next morning he went
to market where he bought a string of ring rolls
and a large stewing rabbit.

On the way home, he stopped by the stream
and pulled up one of his basket fish traps.
Inside were many fine fish.

These he took out,
and in their place
he put the rabbit.

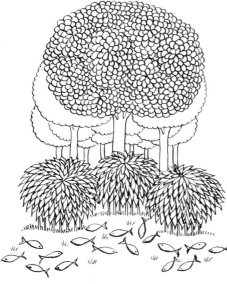

Farther on, he scattered
the fish under some bushes
in the forest.

And finally he hung
the ring rolls on an
old pear tree that
stood at the edge
of the forest.

Now Tomas was ready. He went home and said to Tusya, "Come, woman, let's go to the forest and gather some fish."

Tusya was astonished. "What do you say, husband?" she asked. "Fish in the forest?"

"Why not? Why not?" said Tomas. "Come, let's be off."

Tusya did not know what to think, but off she went. And when they came to the forest, sure enough, there were the fish, lying under the bushes.

"You see," said Tomas. "Didn't I tell you?"

For once Tusya could not say a word. She just gathered up the fish.

"And now," said Tomas, "let's go to the stream. Perhaps a rabbit is caught in one of my fish traps."

"That surely is madness!" exclaimed Tusya. "How could a rabbit get into your fish trap?"

"You didn't expect to find fish in the forest," said Tomas, "and yet you did. Come now, let's go."

And so they went.

But before they came to the fish traps, at the edge of the forest, they happened upon the old pear tree, laden with ring rolls. Tusya shouted with surprise:

"Husband! Husband! Do you see? Ring rolls on a pear tree!"

"Yes," said Tomas. "Is that so strange?"

"But how can it be?" asked Tusya. "Do ring rolls really grow on a pear tree?"

"Don't be silly. Of course not," said Tomas. "They are only hanging on the tree. A cloud of ring rolls must have passed over, and these got caught on the branches."

"Well then, husband, let's shake them down."

So they shook down the ring rolls, gathered them on to a string, and moved on to the stream.

There Tomas hauled in the first trap. Nothing. He hauled in another trap. Still nothing. Then he pulled out the final trap—and inside was the rabbit!

"Och, what a day!" screeched Tusya. "A rabbit in a fish trap! Never since the day I was born have I seen such a thing."

"You've never seen such a thing?" asked Tomas, calmly. "Then look closely. For it's time to go home."

They gathered up the things they had found and started home. But all the way Tusya kept muttering, "Never, never, never have I seen such things: fish in the forest; ring rolls on a pear tree; a rabbit in the fish trap!"

"Why such things are nothing at all," said Tomas finally. "The really strange thing is that I have found a great pot of gold."

"What?"

"I found a great pot of gold."

"And did you now?" said Tusya, not believing him. "Then where is it?"

"Right here," said Tomas, showing Tusya the gold.

"Oh," she exclaimed, "my dearest husband, we'll be rich!"

"Yes," sighed Tomas, "but not for long. When the landowner or his steward finds out, one of them will surely claim it."

"But how will they find out? You can be sure I will never tell," said Tusya.

"Be that as you say," said Tomas. "We must be very careful, dear wife. We must tell no one, or it will go badly with us. We must also be very quiet about our luck in the forest and the stream. Anyone who hears about such things, will also guess that I have found the pot of gold."

"Oh, that is quite certain," said Tusya. "You can be sure that I will tell no one in the world."

On the very same day, toward evening, there came a great noise from the village. Tusya was curious and ran for the window, determined to see what was happening.

"Oh, don't go to look," said Tomas. "It's something most unpleasant, I assure you."

"Do you know what it is then?" asked Tusya.

"Of course," said Tomas, trying not to smile and thinking as fast as he could. "Our distinguished steward has stolen some sausages from our landowner, and he is being chased through the village and beaten with the sausages so he will never steal again."

"So, is that how it is!" said Tusya, believing every word of the story. "Well, I must tell this news to our neighbor Melanka."

"No, you'd better stay home," said Tomas. "Surely you know the ways of our steward. If he heard that you had carried such tales about him, he'd take away our cabbages."

Tusya did as she was told and did not go. She also kept silence about the gold for two whole days.

But finally she could stand it not one minute longer. She ran over to neighbor Melanka.

"Good morning, neighbor," she said, and sat down. She didn't know quite how to begin. "What a lovely day," she went on finally. "But how unfortunate it is to be poor. I had hoped to have new boots for the holidays, but as yet we have no money to get them."

"What's true is true, neighbor," said Melanka.

"Och, yes," said Tusya, "And it's true we may not be poor for long."

"How's that?" asked Melanka, whose ears were already stretching.

"Well, neighbor, I don't quite know how to tell you."

"What is it? Do say," urged Melanka.

"But my husband said I must not tell anyone. Anyone!"

"Dear Tusya, you know I am as silent as the wall!"

"Well, good Melanka," began Tusya, "this is
for your ears alone, and must not be told to
anyone, not anyone else...." And so Tusya told
about the pot of gold.

Tusya was hardly beyond the gate, when
Melanka had on her coat and was running over to
neighbor Paulina.

"Dear neighbor, have you heard…" began Melanka.

Neighbor Natalka was visiting. And so the story of the pot of gold spread.

It wasn't many days before Tomas was called to the village meeting hall and brought before the steward.

"I order you to bring me the pot of gold you have found!" the steward demanded.

"Gold, sir? What gold?" said Tomas.

"Your wife says that you have found a great pot of gold."

"Och, what my wife doesn't say!" Tomas answered, laughing. "If there were no stories to be told in all the earth, my wife could invent as many as were needed."

"We'll see about that!" said the steward. "Bring the wife here."

When Tusya arrived, the steward demanded, "Tell me, did your husband find a pot of gold?"

"Well, sir, yes, sir, he did, sir."

"Now what do you say?" the steward roared at Tomas.

"Perhaps you should ask her when this was, sir," said Tomas.

"Let's see," Tusya tried to recall. "It was the day we went for a walk and gathered fish in the forest. And a cloud of ring rolls was passing and got caught in the pear tree, but we shook them down. Then we found a rabbit in our fish trap..."

Tomas interrupted. "Tell him exactly what day it was, dear wife. Something he will remember."

"It was the day, honored sir, that you were chased through the village," she told the steward.

"The day I was what!" shouted the steward.

"Well, excuse me, sir, but if you ask I must say it. It was when you were beaten with the sausages you had stolen."

The steward was furious. "Have a care what you say there, woman," he roared. "It's a good lashing you need to keep you from making up such stories."

Tomas spoke up at once, pleading for his wife and saying she really was quite unable to tell what the truth was at all.

The steward thought a bit and decided finally that Tomas was right. Tusya could not tell the truth if she tried. And he let both of them go.

So Tomas and Tusya walked home; he laughing to himself in his mustache and she sadly hanging her head, realizing that she had been fooled. By the time they reached home, she was in tears.

"How could you make such a fool of me?" she asked.

"Tusya, my beloved wife," explained Tomas, "it was not I who made a fool of you. It was you who did it yourself. It was your flapping tongue, saying things much better left unsaid. Now let us make up our quarrel and decide how we will use our gold."

So Tusya learned at last that too much talking can cause more trouble than it's worth. And Tusya and Tomas lived on for a long time, happily, peacefully and prosperously.